GHOSTS!

GHOSTLY TALES FROM FOLKLORE

retold by Alvin Schwartz
illustrated by Victoria Chess

SCHOLASTIC INC.

New York Toronto London Auckland Sydney

ISBN 0-590-45710-1

Text copyright © 1991 by Alvin Schwartz.
Illustrations copyright © 1991 by Victoria Chess.
All rights reserved. Published by Scholastic Inc.,
730 Broadway, New York, NY 10003, by arrangement with
HarperCollins Publishers.

12 11 10 9 8 7 6 5 4 3 2 1   3 4 5 6 7 8/9

Printed in the U.S.A.   23

First Scholastic printing, October 1993

"The Umbrella" is adapted from "The Remembrance Service" in *The Doctor to the Dead: Grotesque Legends & Folk Tales of Old Charleston* by John Bennett with permission of Russell & Volkening, as agents for the author.
Copyright 1943, renewed 1971 by John Bennett.

CONTENTS

Do you believe in ghosts?

Some people do.

And the stories

they tell about them

are strange and scary

and fun.

THE HAUNTED HOUSE

There was a big old house

where nobody lived.

Everyone said

it was a haunted house.

"Let's go inside,"

David said to his sister, Ann.

"We are not supposed to," she said.

"Don't be a scaredy-cat," he said.

"It would be fun!"

At last Ann said okay.

David and Ann walked

through the empty, dusty house.

"There is nothing here," Ann said.

"Let's go home."

"Wait," said David,

"I want to see

what is behind that door."

David opened the door

and walked into the room.

Ann waited a few seconds.

Then she sneaked in after him.

"BOO!" she shouted.

David screamed.

"It is only me, silly," Ann said.

"I know," David whispered,

"but what is that behind you?"

SUSIE

Mr. Smith sold cats.

People came from all over

to buy them.

13

"Look at that beautiful cat,"

Nan said to her mother.

"That is the one I want."

She pointed to a cat

sitting on the cash register.

"What is that cat's name?"

Nan asked Mr. Smith.

"Susie," he said.

"How much does she cost?"

asked Nan's mother.

"Susie is not for sale,"

said Mr. Smith.

15

"But I want to give her to Nan
for her birthday,"
Nan's mother said.
"I cannot sell Susie,"
Mr. Smith said.
"I will give you fifty dollars,"
Nan's mother said.

"I could not sell her

even if I wanted to,"

Mr. Smith said.

Susie purred.

Nan reached out to pet her.

17

Her hand went right through the cat.

"There is nothing there!"

Nan screamed.

18

"I should have told you,"

said Mr. Smith.

"Susie died a year ago.

But she comes back to visit

now and then."

A LITTLE GREEN BOTTLE

Kate was the biggest bully
in school.

She liked to pick on Joe
because he was so small.

"Joe! Give me your lunch,"
Kate would shout.

Joe would be so scared
he would hand it right over.

But one day Kate said,

"Joe! Give me your new bicycle."

Joe was so upset,

he told his teacher.

Kate got into

a lot of trouble.

"I am going to get you for this!"

Kate told Joe.

But Kate never got the chance.

23

She suddenly got sick and died.

The day after she died,

her ghost whispered in Joe's ear,

"I am *still* going to get you."

Kate's ghost began to haunt Joe.

It hid in his desk at school,

and whispered scary things to him.

It jumped out at him

from behind trees.

It made horrible faces at him
at night.

One day

while Joe was eating,

the ghost rode his bicycle

back and forth across the table.

"Kate, please stop!"

Joe begged.

"Never!" the ghost screamed.

It turned itself into an angry bull.

"How did you do that?"

Joe asked.

"I can do anything I want,"

said the ghost.

It got bigger and bigger—and bigger.

Soon it filled the room.

That gave Joe an idea.

"Kate," he said,

"can you make yourself very small?"

"Of course," said the ghost.

Joe pointed to

a little green bottle

on the table.

"Can you make yourself

small enough to jump into this?"

he asked.

"Of course," said the ghost,

and it jumped into the bottle.

Joe grabbed a cork

and pushed it into the bottle.

Then he threw the bottle

into the river.

The river carried it to the ocean.

The bottle floated away.

Kate's ghost

has not been heard from since.

But if you ever see

a little green bottle

washed up on the beach,

36

DON'T OPEN IT!!

THE UMBRELLA

One night George heard
people singing in the cemetery.
He went inside to listen.
"We are singing to the dead,"
one of the singers told him.
"Sometimes people forget
about them."

The song was so beautiful

George joined in.

It was raining,

but everybody kept on singing.

One of the singers

handed George an umbrella.

"This will keep your voice

nice and dry,"

she said.

They sang a few more songs.

Then they stopped—

and vanished.

"Ghosts!" George cried out,

and he ran.

He ran all the way home.

When he got home,

he still was holding the umbrella

the ghost had given him.

George used it until the day he died.

Then the umbrella vanished.

THREE LITTLE GHOSTS

There were three little ghosts

Sitting on posts

Eating buttered toast.

They had butter on their fists

Running down their wrists,

Butter on their sheets

Running down their feet.

What slobs!

THE TEENY-TINY WOMAN

Once there was a teeny-tiny woman

who lived all alone

in a teeny-tiny house.

One day she went

for a teeny-tiny walk.

And on that walk

she came to a teeny-tiny graveyard.

And in that graveyard

she saw a teeny-tiny grave.

And on that grave

she found a set of teeny-tiny teeth.

"Look at those teeth!"

said the teeny-tiny woman

in her teeny-tiny voice.

"Just what I need,"

and she popped them

right into her teeny-tiny mouth.

Then she went home

and took a teeny-tiny nap.

Soon she heard

a teeny-tiny voice calling,

"GIVE ME BACK MY TEETH!

I WANT MY TEETH!"

53

She hid her teeny-tiny head
under her teeny-tiny blanket
and closed her teeny-tiny eyes.

But again the voice called,

"GIVE ME BACK MY TEETH!

I WANT MY TEETH!"

This scared the teeny-tiny woman

so much

she threw

the teeny-tiny teeth

out her teeny-tiny window.

"KEEP YOUR TEENY-TINY TEETH!"

the teeny-tiny woman shouted.

The teeny-tiny voice shouted back,

"AND YOU KEEP

YOUR TEENY-TINY HANDS OFF

MY TEENY-TINY TEETH!"

Then the teeny-tiny woman heard
teeny-tiny footsteps
run back to the graveyard.

GHOST, GET LOST

If a ghost ever scares you,

just say,

"Crisscross, double-cross,

Ghost, get lost!"

And it will go away.